MARK TEAGUE

FIREHOUSE!

SCHOLASTIC INC.

New York Toronto London Auckland
Sydney Mexico City New Delhi Hong Kong

ISBN 978-0-545-39973-9

Text and illustrations copyright © 2010 by Mark Teague. All rights reserved. Published by Orchard Books, an imprint of Scholastic Inc. ORCHARD BOOKS and design are registered trademarks of Watts Publishing Group, Ltd., used under license. SCHOLASTIC and associated logos are trademarks and/or registered trademarks of Scholastic Inc.

12 11 10 9 8 7 6 5 4 3   15 16 17 18 19/0
Printed in the U.S.A.   40

First Scholastic paperback printing, October 2011

The artwork was created using oil paints.
The text was set in Eagle Book.
Book design by Charles Kreloff

Edward wants to be a firefighter.
One day he and Judy visit a firehouse.

Edward tries on a shiny red fire hat.

Mrs. Speckle, the fire chief, shows them around.
"First you can help wash the fire truck," she says.
"Later we will have a practice fire drill."

Everyone helps.
"A clean fire engine is a happy fire engine," says a firefighter.

Edward climbs into the driver's seat.
He steers to the right. He steers to the left.

"This is where we live,"
says a firefighter.

Suddenly, the alarm rings!

"This is a fire drill," calls the fire chief.
The firefighters spring into action!

Everyone hurries down the fire pole.

"Hang on, Edward!" a firefighter calls.
The fire engine speeds away.

Judy opens the fire hydrant.
The water is so strong it knocks Edward off his feet.

Everyone works together.

Edward practices going up the ladder.

But he needs help coming down.
Lifesaving is a firefighter's most important job.

They return to the firehouse.
After lunch, the alarm rings again.
This time, it is a real emergency!

A kitten is stuck up a tree!
"Who will save her?" asks a firefighter.
Edward volunteers, "Let me!"

Edward climbs the ladder and rescues the kitten.
"Good work!" the firefighters cheer.

Edward saves the day.
There is a big parade to celebrate.

A firefighter needs rest.
It is bedtime at the firehouse.